THE USBORNE BOOK OF
EASY KEYBOARD TUNES

Philip Hawthorn and Anthony Marks

Edited by Jenny Tyler

Designed by Kim Blundell and Philip Hawthorn

Illustrated by Kim Blundell

Technical consultant: Daniel Scott

Original music by Sharon Armstrong, revised and adapted for keyboard by Daniel Scott

Music engraving by Poco Ltd., Letchworth, Herts

Contents

About this book

This is a book of tunes that you can play on your electronic keyboard instrument or your piano. It will help you to improve your skill as a player, and also to read and understand music better.

In this book there are folk songs, tunes from classical music and jazz tunes. Some you won't have heard before because they have been specially written. There are also tunes for two players.

The tunes get harder as you go through the book. For the first few tunes you do not need to move the position of your hands as you play, and you only use one note at a time. The tunes at the end are more difficult.

Some pieces of music contain signs, symbols or words that you may not have seen before. Every time a new music symbol or word appears, it will be explained in a box at the foot of the page.

The first electric keyboard instrument was invented at the beginning of the 20th century. Since that time many amazing instruments have been made. You can find out about these on some of the pages in this book.

You will find lots of interesting facts about the tunes in this book, and about composers and types of music. There is also a section at the back about recordings you can listen to if you want to hear more keyboard music.

Starting to play

This page tells you some of the things you need to know before you start to play. At first it may seem difficult to remember everything at the same time, but if you keep practising you will find that it gets easier very quickly.

If you play for a little while every day, you will remember what you have learned.

The keyboard

The keyboard is made up of groups of white and black keys. Each key plays a different note, and each note has a name. The first pieces in this book use the white notes only. This picture shows the names of the white notes on the keyboard.

This note is called middle C. It is the C nearest to the middle of the keyboard.

F G A B C D E F G

Writing music down

Music is written on sets of five lines. Each set is called a stave* Notes are written on the lines and in the spaces between them. Each line or space matches a note on the keyboard. A sign called a clef at the front of the stave tells you where on the keyboard to play. These staves show where each note is written on the music.

Treble clef

This note is middle C.

C D E F G

F G A B C

Bass clef

Left hand notes on this stave.

Right hand notes on this stave.

Finger numbers

Each tune in this book has numbers above the music to tell you which fingers to use to play each note. This picture shows which number stands for which finger. For the first few tunes in this book, you start with your thumbs on middle C.

Now you can begin playing the piece on the opposite page, "Sur le pont d'Avignon". You will also need to read the section called "Counting" below the music. It will tell you how long you have to hold each note to make the music sound right.

In North America, a set of five lines is called a staff.

Sur le pont d'Avignon

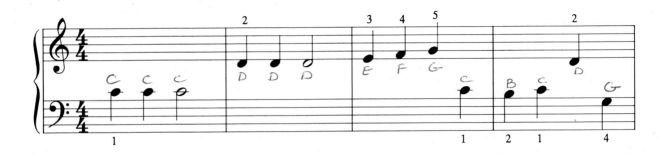

Counting

When you play, you need to know how long to hold each note. The length of a note is counted in units called beats. You have to count beats steadily and evenly. Three types of note are shown here. Each one lasts a different number of beats*.

A semibreve (or whole note): 4 beats (count "1, 2, 3, 4").

A minim (or half note): 2 beats (count "1, 2").

A crotchet (or quarter note) (count "1").

4 beats

2 beats

1 beat

Time signatures

The numbers at the start of each tune are called the time signature. A time signature tells you how many beats there are in each bar of the piece, and the length of the beats. (For most of the pieces in this book, the lower number is 4, as each beat is a crotchet long.)

The top number tells you that there are four beats in every bar.

The lower number tells you that each beat is a crotchet long.

*The names in brackets are what the notes are called in North America.

5

Bobby Shaftoe

This is an English folk song. It was written around 1760, about a man who goes to sea.

trumpet/march

Sounds and styles

Keyboards can make sounds like other instruments, and play rhythms. At the start of most pieces in this book you will find ideas about which sound and rhythm to use*.

For this piece, select the "trumpet" sound.

Then press the button for a "march" rhythm.

You can find out more about choosing sounds and rhythms on page 62.

Up and down

This tune has dotted minims in it. You can find out about them below.

In this piece there are three crotchet beats in each bar. Count "1, 2, 3" as you play.

violin/waltz

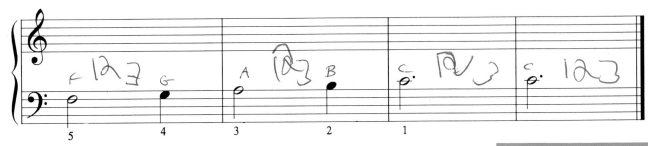

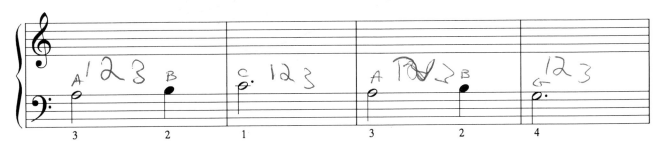

Dotted minims

A dot after a note increases its length by half as much again. A minim lasts for two beats, so a dot adds one beat to its length.

A minim is two beats long.

Half a minim is one beat.

A dotted minim is three beats.

The waltz is a dance rhythm with three beats in a bar.

Choosing a sound

Some sounds on the keyboard last as long as you hold the key down. Others fade quickly. *Legato* pieces need sounds that you can hold.

The dinosaur and the dormouse

Rests

A rest can appear on either stave. It tells you to stop playing with that hand for a certain number of beats. Here are three types of rest.

Semibreve rest (4 beats)*

Minim rest (2 beats)

Crotchet rest (1 beat)

*This symbol is also used to show a whole bar rest of any number of beats.

9

Two o'clock

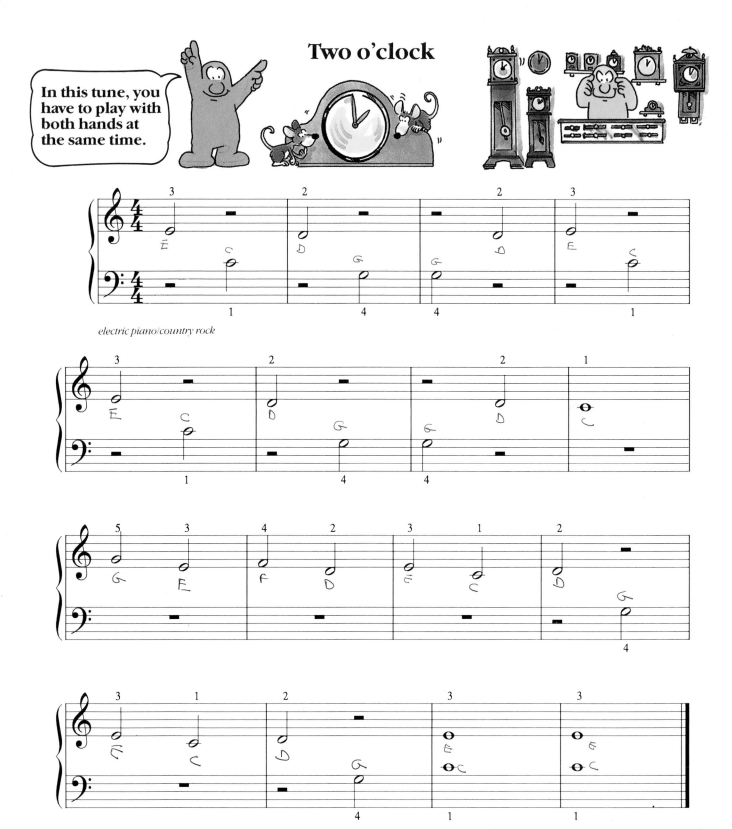

In this tune, you have to play with both hands at the same time.

electric piano/country rock

Keeping time

When you play music, you must keep a steady beat. You can use the rhythms on your keyboard to help you, but it helps to learn pieces without them first. When you know the piece, choose a rhythm and adjust the speed so that you can play along with it easily.

A new note

The semibreve has no stem. It lasts for four beats.

Girls and boys come out to play

Tying notes together

Notes on the same line or space can be tied together to make one long note. This has the same number of beats as the other ones added together.

This is called a tie.

A black note

The black note in this tune is the one below B. It is called B flat. In the music it has a ♭ in front of it.

This tune has another black note in it. You can find out about it at the bottom of the page.

The bell ringers

tubular bells/8-beat

Another black note

The black note in this tune is called F sharp. It is the one above the F note and has a sharp sign, ♯, in front of it.

Put the fourth finger of your right hand on the F♯ note before you play.

Accidentals

A sharp or flat before a note is called an accidental. You play the note sharp or flat each time it appears in that bar. The barline cancels the effect of the accidental.

Here is another accidental, the natural. It is used to cancel a flat or a sharp.

13

Apache rain dance

When you play this tune, you will have to change your hand positions.

The finger numbers tell you where to put your hands.

trumpet/8-beat

Quavers

A quaver is half a crotchet beat long. Clap the rhythm on the right as you say the words. Both quavers are the same length, so try not to rush them.

Quick   qua - ver   claps

Quavers can also be written singly, like this.

Folk dance

Choosing a sound

To play *staccato*, you will need to choose a short sound that fades as soon as you take your finger off the key.

Mountain song

The tunes on these pages have letters to tell you how loudly or softly to play.

The letters stand for Italian words. You can find out about them below.

trumpet/8-beat

Loud and soft

The signs for loud and soft are based on the Italian words *forte* (loud) and *piano* (soft).

forte (*f*) means loud.

mezzo-forte (*mf*) means quite loud.

mezzo-piano (*mp*) means fairly quiet.

piano (*p*) means quiet.

16

Away in a manger

This tune has letters in it to tell you to play softly.

This tune* was written by William Kirkpatrick, an American composer.

electric piano/no rhythm

Playing loudly

On large keyboards the harder you press the keys, the louder the notes sound. On small keyboards you must find other ways of altering the volume.

Some keyboards have a footpedal to change the volume.

Or you can use the volume switches on the control panel.

Or reset the machine and choose a louder or softer sound.

*This is the tune most commonly used in Britain.

17

Haunted house

This piece contains dotted crotchets. Find out what they mean below.

organ/8-beat

Dotted crotchets

A dotted crotchet is one and a half beats long. Here you can see how to play the right rhythm.

1　2　&　3　4

The half beat here is a quaver.

Getting louder and softer

This sign tells you to get louder bit by bit.

This sign tells you to get quieter a little at a time.

18

At the fair

Joining notes together

When notes are linked by a curved line, it means you have to join them together smoothly. This is called playing *legato*.

Where, oh where has my little dog gone?

This song, first sung in the late 1800s, was also known as "The Dutchman's Wee Dog".

clarinet/waltz

Two notes together

When you play more than one note at a time with one hand, it is called a chord. Here are some finger exercises to help you play chords more easily.

Repeat the music until you can play it smoothly.

20

Down in the valley

How fast to play

Words written at the beginning of a tune tell you at what speed you have to play. Sometimes the words are in Italian. This is because music was first printed in Italy. Below are some words for different tempos.

Very fast Presto

Fast Allegro

Walking pace Andante

Slowly Lento

Repeating music from the beginning

The sign below is called a repeat mark. It means you go back to the beginning and play the piece again.

The last bar of this tune is the only one you do not play twice.

You ignore the repeat mark the second time round.

The grand old duke of York

There are sharp signs at the start of this tune. Find out more below.

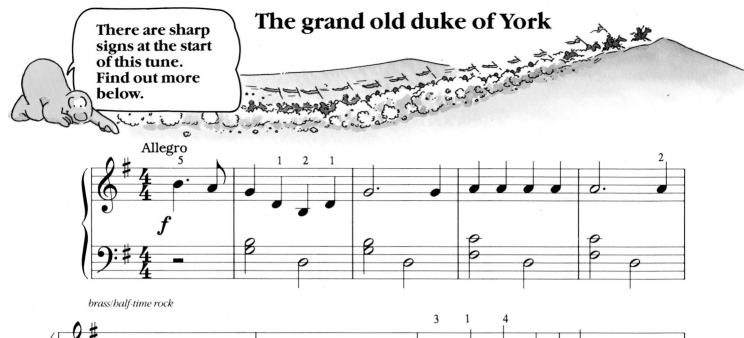

Allegro

brass/half-time rock

Key signatures

The ♯ sign next to the clefs is called a key signature. You play F♯ instead of F all the way through this piece, except when there are accidentals.

The key signature saves you writing a ♯ sign every time there is an F.

The flat and natural signs in this piece are accidentals, and only apply to the bar in which they appear. The natural signs cancel the effect of the F♯ in the key signature.

22

Lavender's blue

electric piano/waltz

Amazing keyboards

One of the first electric musical instruments was the Telharmonium. It was invented in 1906 by an American called Thaddeus Cahill.

Anna's gerbils

You can find out what *allegro* means on page 21.

Watch out for the accidentals in this tune!

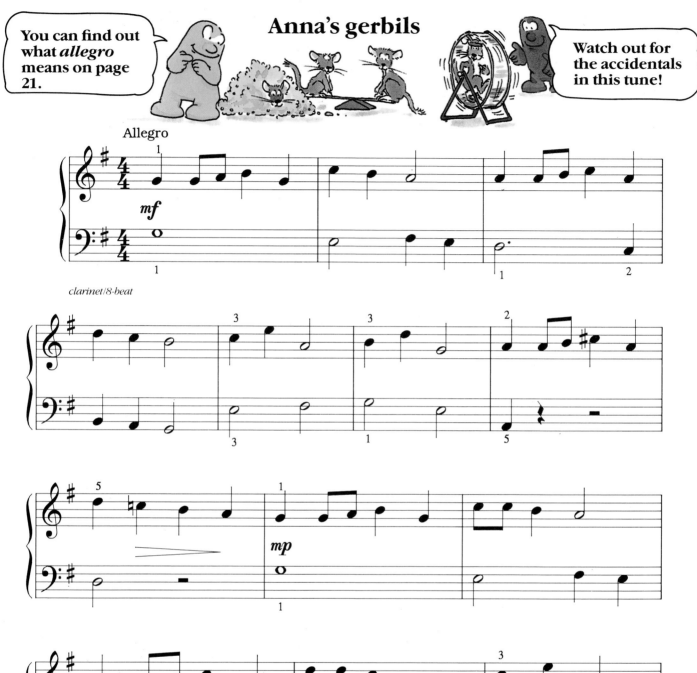

Allegro

clarinet/8-beat

mf

mp

German national anthem

This tune was written by an Austrian called Haydn (see pages 48-49).

It was adopted as the German national anthem in 1922.

Allegro

strings/no rhythm

We wish you a merry Christmas

This carol was written in England at the end of the 19th century.

It became very popular in America in the late 1930s.

Allegro

trumpet/waltz

Making sounds

Keyboard instruments use electricity in many different ways to produce sounds. Methods of sound production have changed over the years, so that very small electronic instruments can now make many more sounds than larger keyboards used to.

The Hammond organ was invented in the 1930s and became popular with jazz musicians. It contains small rotating discs to make the sounds.

The Telharmonium (see page 23) used huge spinning cylinders to create sounds.

The Mellotron was popular in the 1970s. It contained short tape recordings of notes played by various instruments. When the player pressed a key, the tape replayed the sound.

Burger bar blues

Space walk rag

Like blues, rags were developed by black Americans in the last century.

The sign ⅞ is a quaver rest. Pause for half a beat.

Playing rag rhythms

Rags have a special rhythm, known as ragtime. Here are some hints to help you play ragtime well.

When you play, try not to rush. Make the music sound very relaxed and keep a steady beat.

Hold the second and fourth beats of the bar slightly longer than the others.

The slightly jerky rhythm is called syncopation.

29

Au clair de la lune

This tune was written in about 1680 by a French composer called Lully.

The title is French. It means "by the light of the moon".

flute/8-beat

Amazing keyboards

In the 1920s inventors in Europe and America produced many electric keyboards. But many of these instruments were very fragile and could only play one note at a time.

Frère Jacques

This type of tune is called a round. Find out more below.

The title is French for "Brother James".

A

mf

oboe/8-beat

B

How to play a round

A round is a tune that several people can play or sing, each starting a few bars apart. The different parts blend together.

To play this round, one person starts at the beginning. The second player starts at the beginning when the first person reaches the letter B.

The first player starts playing on his own.

The second finishes playing on her own.

Two people playing on one keyboard

If two people play on one keyboard, this picture shows you which notes each of them should play.

Middle C

Player 1

Player 2

Playing a round by yourself

You can play both parts by yourself. Many keyboards have a section called a sequencer that lets you record your playing. Or you can use a tape recorder.

First, record yourself playing the tune.

Then play it back and join in when the recorded part gets to B.

31

Walking

More about phrases

Some music is written in sections called phrases, like words are spoken in sentences. Lift your hand slightly between each phrase. It is a bit like taking a breath.

This piece was written by an Austrian composer called Antonio Diabelli (1781-1858).

Auld lang syne

Clementine

piano/waltz

Dotted quavers

A dot after a quaver increases it by half as much again. Half a quaver is called a semiquaver. A dotted quaver lasts for three semiquavers. Semiquavers can be written in several ways.

34   *See page 62 for an explanation of the symbol ♩

Oh, Susannah

Amazing instruments

The *ondes martenot* was invented in France in the 1920s by a man called Maurice Martenot. It was one of the first successful electronic keyboard instruments, and is still being made today.

Amazing keyboards

In the 1960s several inventors developed instruments called synthesizers. They were able to make many different sounds, but were monophonic (only able to play one note at a time).

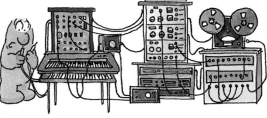

Most early synthesizers were several separate boxes (called modules) that had to be linked together by wires.

Dvořák wrote the symphony while he was living in New York.

At that time, many Europeans thought of America as a "new world".

Parts of the symphony are based on American Indian folk music, spirituals and rags.

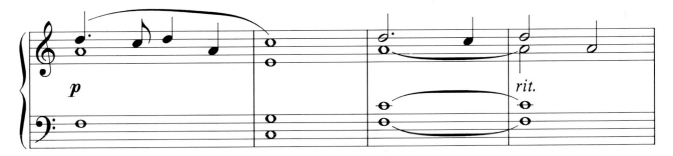

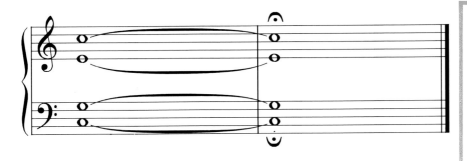

Slowing down
The word *rit.* is short for *ritardando*, Italian for "holding back". It means "get slower bit by bit".

When you reach the *rit.* sign, count and play more slowly until you get to the end.

Sometimes the word *rallentando* (or *rall.*) is used instead (see page 51).

In 1970 an American called Robert Moog invented the Minimoog. It was the first portable synthesizer, and is one of the most popular keyboards ever made.

37

Autumn

This tune is in 6/8 time. There are six quavers in each bar, in two groups of three.

Cantabile is an Italian word. It means play smoothly and expressively, as if you were singing.

Cantabile

electric piano/rock-and-roll

rit. _ _ _ _ _

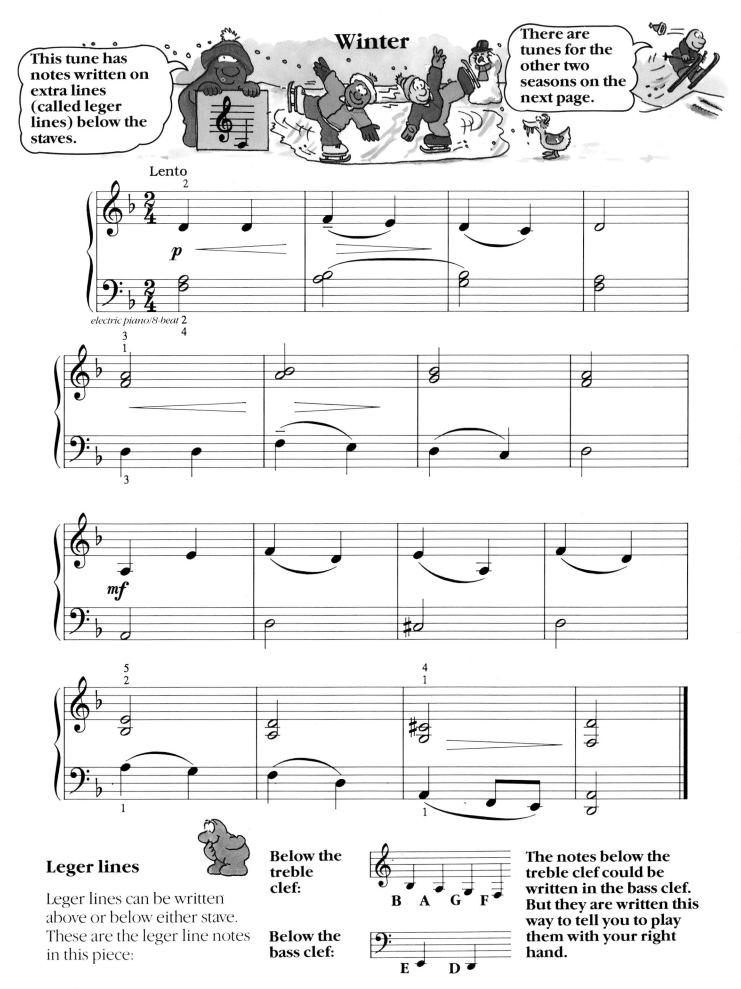

This tune has notes written on extra lines (called leger lines) below the staves.

Winter

There are tunes for the other two seasons on the next page.

Lento

electric piano/8-beat

Leger lines

Leger lines can be written above or below either stave. These are the leger line notes in this piece:

Below the treble clef:

B   A   G   F

Below the bass clef:

E   D

The notes below the treble clef could be written in the bass clef. But they are written this way to tell you to play them with your right hand.

39

Spring

Look out for the echo in this piece. One section is played *mezzo forte*, then repeated *piano*.

Allegro

harpsichord/8-beat

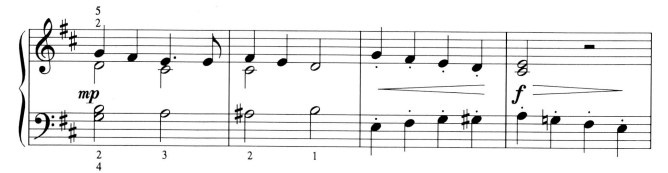

Four seasons

The tunes on these four pages were written to sound like the four seasons. Other composers have also done this, including Vivaldi and Haydn.

Test your friends. Tell them the tunes you are going to play are based on the four seasons.

Play them in any order. Afterwards, see if they can guess the titles.

40

Summer

There are new leger line notes in this piece. See below.

More leger line notes

In this piece there are two leger line notes above the right hand stave and two above the left hand stave.

B **A**

D **E**

Remember that key signatures and accidentals apply to leger lines as well as to notes on the stave.

41

Wedding march

This tune was written in 1842 by a German composer called Mendelssohn. It is often played at weddings as the bride enters the church.

You have to repeat part of this tune. See below.

organ/8-beat

Fine

D.C. al Fine

A new kind of repeat

Fine (pronounced "fee-nay") is Italian for "the end". *D. C.* stands for *Da Capo*. *Da Capo al Fine* means play from the top until you reach the *Fine* sign.

Start at the beginning and play through the piece once until you reach *D. C. al Fine*.

Then go back to the top and play through to the *Fine* sign.

The thick barline shows you where to stop playing.

FINE

Daisy Bell

*See page 62 for an explanation of the symbol >

Nobody knows the trouble I've seen

Spirituals

Spirituals were first sung in America in the middle of the last century, usually by black slaves.

Kum by yah

This tune is another spiritual.

The title means "come by here".

Making sounds

The sounds of many synthesizers (see page 36) and other keyboards are made by electronic devices called oscillators. Like the strings of a violin, or the skin of a drum, oscillators are the part of the instrument that produces the sound. Oscillators work in different ways.

In some early synthesizers, electric signals were used to control the oscillators. But if the electric power varied, the oscillators went out of tune.

Later synthesizers are based on microchips. All the sounds come from computer information. Part of the microchip acts as an oscillator.

The microchips in modern keyboards store huge amounts of information. This is why instruments today can make so many different sounds at once.

Riding on a donkey

Allegretto means "not quite as fast as allegro".

Parts of the left hand of this piece imitate bagpipes.

Computers and keyboards

Many modern keyboards can be linked to computers using a special system called MIDI (Musical Instrument Digital Interface).

With some computer programs you can write music on the computer and play it back on a keyboard.

Toreador's song

This tune is from an opera (find out more below) called "Carmen". A toreador is a bullfighter.

"Carmen" was written by Bizet, a French composer who lived from 1838 to 1875.

Allegro

trumpet/march

Opera

An opera is like a play except that nearly all the words are sung.

There is an orchestra in front of the stage to play the music.

Operas were first written around the year 1600. Many composers have written operas, based on many different stories. Famous opera composers include Mozart and Verdi.

St Anthony Chorale

Composer file

48　*See page 62 for an explanation of the symbol ♩*

From the "Surprise" Symphony

First and second time bars

The two bars with brackets over them in this piece are called the first time bar and the second time bar. Here is how to play them.

We three kings

The 3/8 time signature means there are three quaver beats in each bar.

This sign tells you to pause. Find out more below.

This carol was written in the mid-1800s by an American clergyman.

harp/slow rock

mf

mp

rall._ _ _ _ _ _ _ _ _ _

Pause

When you see this sign above the music, you have to pause for a second or so.

Keep your fingers on the keys while you pause.

Pauses are often in song tunes, between the verse and the chorus.

This tune continues on the next page.

50

Find out what *rall.* and *a tempo* mean below.

In the Bible it says that Jesus was visited by some kings. It doesn't say there were three, though.

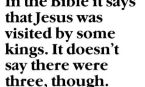

a tempo

Rallentando and *a tempo*

Rallentando means "slowing down gradually" It is often just written as *rall*.

A tempo means you go back to the speed you were playing before.

Sometimes the word *ritardando* (or *rit.*) is used instead. It means the same thing.

Lullaby

Small notes

These small notes are called grace notes. You play them as quickly as you can.

Rock-a-bye baby

This lullaby was probably written in about 1629 by one of the first European settlers in America.

It was inspired by the way American Indians hung their cradles on tree branches.

Andante

piano/waltz

Sampling keyboards

Some computers can record natural sounds very accurately. Sounds are stored as computer information called samples and can be played back from a keyboard.

Samplers were originally used to reproduce the sound of musical instruments.

But they can also be used to record and play back any other sound.

53

From Symphony no.7
(third movement)

When this symphony was first performed in 1812, the audience cheered so much that the orchestra played some parts again.

Find out what *allegretto* means on page 46.

55

Scarborough fair

This tune is an old English folk song.

Andante

harp/waltz

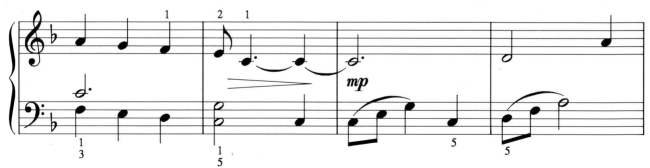

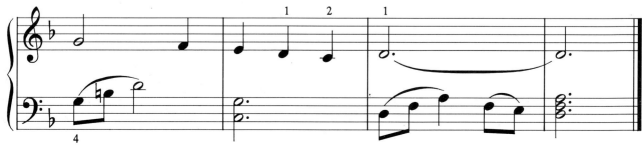

56

From "Pomp and Circumstance"

A classic duet (part B)

Octaves and scales

An octave is the distance from any note to the next one with the same name. A scale is a set of eight notes played one after the other covering an octave.

Melody in A minor (part B)

This is another duet, based on a South American dance rhythm called the bossa nova.

Remember that the music on this page has both hands in the bass clef.

piano/bossa nova

Melody in A minor
(part A)

Music help

On this page you can see all the music symbols and words that are used in the rest of the book. The index on page 64 will show you where everything is explained.

How loudly to play

This list contains symbols and instructions about how loudly or softly to play.

pp	*(pianissimo)*	very softly
p	*(piano)*	softly
mp	*(mezzo-piano)*	quite softly
mf	*(mezzo-forte)*	quite loudly
f	*(forte)*	loudly
ff	*(fortissimo)*	very loudly

How fast to play

Here are the Italian words that tell you how quickly or slowly to play.

presto	**very fast**
allegro	**fast**
allegretto	**not too fast**
andante	**"walking pace" (quite slowly)**
lento	**very slowly**
ritardando, rallentando	**gradually slowing down**
a tempo	**return to original speed**

Music symbols

Here are other special symbols you will find in the book.

pause	⌒	**repeats**
tie		**slur**
semibreve	o	**semibreve rest**
minim	♩	**minim rest**
crotchet	♩	**crotchet rest**
quaver	♪	**quaver rest**
semiquaver	♬	**semiquaver rest**
sharp ♯	**flat** ♭	**natural** ♮
grace notes		**dotted note**
staccato		**octave** 8 − − − − − − −⌐
accent		(play this note slightly louder than the ones around it)
stress mark		(play this note with more emphasis, or hold it for slightly longer)

About sounds and styles

Nearly all electronic keyboards can make many different sounds. Most of them play rhythms too. To find out how to make these work, look at the instruction book that came with your own keyboard. Try all the sounds and rhythms until you are familiar with them.

At the start of most pieces in this book you will find ideas about which sound and rhythm to use. (Where there is no idea for a rhythm, it means that the piece will sound best without drums.) If at the start of a piece you see this:

clarinet/march

it means it would be a good idea to use a clarinet sound and a march rhythm. But it is also fun to experiment. Try using different sounds and rhythms for each piece, to see which you like best.

Listening to keyboard music

If you want to play the piano or keyboard well, it helps if you listen to a lot of music. This list contains suggestions of different kinds of music that include keyboards. It also contains recordings of some of the instruments mentioned elsewhere in the book.

Classical music

The most important keyboard instrument in classical music is the piano. There are many recordings of pieces by the classical composers mentioned in this book. Here are the names of some famous pianists to look out for: Claudio Arrau, Daniel Barenboim, Alfred Brendel, Cecile Ousset and Maurizio Pollini.

The piano is often used in 20th century music by composers who were also pianists. The composers Bartók and Stravinsky, for example, wrote many pieces that they first played themselves.

Many composers use electric and electronic keyboard instruments in their music. The *ondes martenot* has a solo part in the Turangalîla Symphony by the French composer Olivier Messiaen, and there are synthesizer and organ parts in music by Stockhausen, Steve Reich and John Adams.

Jazz

Most keyboard players in jazz concentrate on the piano or the electric piano. There are hundreds of excellent jazz pianists who have made recordings; some of the most important are Count Basie, Dave Brubeck, Duke Ellington, Bill Evans, Keith Jarrett, Charles Mingus, Jelly Roll Morton, Oscar Peterson, Cecil Taylor and Fats Waller.

There are also many organists and keyboard players in jazz. Jimmy Smith, Shirley Scott and Jack McDuff are best known for their use of the Hammond organ. The synthesizer and other electronic instruments can be heard on recordings by Chick Corea, Herbie Hancock, Sun Ra, George Duke, the group Weather Report and Miles Davis.

Pop and rock

Many pop and rock groups base their music on synthesizers and electronic drum machines. They include Kraftwerk, the Human League, New Order and Depeche Mode. Other musicians use both electronic and non-electronic instruments, but have prominent keyboards. These include Michael Jackson, Prince, Simple Minds and Eurythmics.

The Mellotron can be heard on *Strawberry Fields for Ever* by the Beatles, and on some recordings by Genesis and the Moody Blues. Jimmy Smith plays a Hammond organ solo on the title track of Michael Jackson's album *Bad*.

Ragtime and blues

Many pianists have made recordings of the rags of Scott Joplin. Among his most famous pieces are "The Entertainer" (used as the soundtrack for the film *The Sting*) and "Maple Leaf Rag".

There are various styles of blues piano. One of the most famous is boogie woogie, which was popular in Chicago in the 1940s. Famous boogie woogie pianists were Jimmy Yancey and Meade "Lux" Lewis. Later blues pianists include Otis Spann and Professor Longhair.

Soul and dance music

Keyboard instruments have always played an important part in soul music. The Hammond organ was used by many groups in the early 1960s. It can be heard, for example, on *Time is Tight* by Booker T. and the MGs, and on many recordings by Al Green. As the synthesizer became more popular in the early 1970s it was used by many groups, including Parliament/Funkadelic, partly to reinforce bass lines. In the late 1970s keyboard parts became a feature of many disco records, such as *Mighty Real* by Sylvester.

Advanced synthesizer technology quickly found its way into soul and dance music in the 1980s. Drum machines are an important element of most rap and hip-hop. Many modern groups, like De la Soul and Deee-lite, also use electronic samples of other recordings. For excellent keyboard arrangements in modern soul music, listen to recordings by Alexander O'Neal produced by Jimmy Jam and Terry Lewis.

Index

Tune titles are shown in **bold type**; foreign
musical terms are shown in *italic* type.

First published in 1991 by Usborne Publishing Ltd, Usborne House, 83-85 Saffron Hill, London EC1N 8RT, England. Copyright © 1991 Usborne Publishing Ltd. The name Usborne and the device are trade marks of Usborne Publishing Ltd. All rights reserved.